This Book Belongs To:

_____

Cameroun, The Majestic Little Africa

Snow Flower and The Panther

To my kids, friends and family who helped me along the way.

ISBN-13: 978-0692109182

First Printing 2018

SnowFlowerBooks.com

NDE MEDIA GROUP

—— NOBILITY, DIGNITY, ELEGANCE ——

Ndemediagroup.com

"There he goes again," sighed Snow Flower. Red was crowing loudly outside her window as the sun rose in the Central Africa sky. "And I was having such a great dream."

Snow stretched in bed, moving her braided hair away from her big brown eyes. Her mother named her after the snow, although it never snowed in Cameroon. Still, her mother believed Snow Flower was as pure as fresh white snow and as beautiful as a flower in full bloom.

Glancing through the window, Snow Flower flung her arms out wide to welcome the new day. "It's going to be another exciting day!" she said out loud.

She caught a whiff of the sweet, vanilla-flavored beignet ("ben-yay"), a type of African doughnut that Snow Flower's grandma often made. Snow Flower hopped out of bed, washed, and put on her favorite yellow dress and her beaded sandals. Then she ran to the outdoor kitchen.

She came up behind her grandma, Mamie Marguerite, and surprised her with a hug. "Good morning, Mamie!"

"Well, good morning, Snow Flower," said Mamie Marguerite as she put more wood on the fire. Then she sat on a stool, dipping clumps of dough into a pot of hot oil. Snow Flower grabbed a fresh, warm beignet from the platter and took a bite. The sugary, fluffy doughnut melted in her mouth and she smiled with satisfaction.

Mamie smiled too. "After you're done eating your beignet, could you go to the river and bring back some water to drink and cook with?"

"Sure, Mamie. I'll be off soon," replied Snow Flower. She grabbed a few more beignets and stuffed two in her pocket.

Licking her fingers, she picked up her calabash for collecting water and skipped down the road toward the river.

"Be careful!" Mamie called out as a car zoomed by.

On the way, Snow Flower stopped at her friend's house and knocked on his front door. "Remi!" she called. Moments later, the door opened and Remi ran outside.

"Hi Snow," he said. "Where are you going?"

"I am going to the river. Do you want to come?" Snow Flower asked.

"Sure," Remi said. He grabbed his water jug and walked alongside Snow Flower.

As they left the village of Bankolo and made for the river, Snow Flower and Remi sang the Cameroon National Anthem, which they were learning in school.

"Land of Promise, land of Glory! Thou, of life and joy…"

In the background, they could hear the calls of local villagers selling their goods along the main road.

Snow remembered the two beignets she had put in her pocket and she gave them to Remi.

"Thanks, Snow Flower," he said as he gratefully ate them.

"Let's take the shortcut through the forest to get to the river," Snow Flower suggested as they reached the forest. It was a hot day, but the Bubinga trees, the tall palm trees, and the banana trees with giant leaves provided shade along the path.

As they walked through the forest, they were startled by a rustle in the low-lying brush ahead.

"Did you hear that, Snow?"
Remi asked, his eyes wide open.

"Yes. What if it's a big snake,
or a hyena, or even a lion," said
Snow. "Let's walk a little faster."

13

Soon enough, they arrived at the river's edge. The water sparkled in the sunlight. They splashed in the cool water and scooped up shiny pebbles from the shallows by the bank.

"Hey, Snow Flower, watch this!" Remi
skipped a rock all the way across the river.

"Let me try," said Snow Flower. She reached
for a rock but touched a frog instead. "Remi,
look! There are so many frogs in the water!"

15

"Let's try to catch one," said Remi. They both leaned down and tried to scoop the small frogs out of the river. "Snow, look! I've caught one!"

Snow Flower reached over and stroked the frog with her finger. It was hot outside, but the frog's skin felt cool and moist. It hopped from Remi's hand into the river with a splash.

"They are so fast," said Snow Flower, laughing at the leaping frogs. "We should get our water and head home."

Remi and Snow Flower filled their water jugs; then Snow balanced her calabash on her head and the two friends headed back to the village.

As they passed through the forest, they heard the rustling in the bushes again.

"Hey, it's the same sound we heard before...let's check it out." Remi gripped his slingshot and Snow Flower placed her calabash on the ground. "Yeah, let's take a look."

They approached the bushes, and Snow Flower peaked through the leaves. "Oh, Remi, it's a young panther!"

The two children spread out the leaves of the bush and peered through at the panther. They could see its shiny black coat and faint brown spots.

"He's stuck in a hunting trap," said Remi.

"Poor thing," said Snow wishing they could help.

Snow approached the panther cautiously, looking around in case his mother was nearby and might try to protect her cub. The panther looked at them with fear in his emerald-green eyes. But he did not back away.

"I think we can undo the trap and free him," said Snow as she leaned forward. The panther growled but she spoke to him gently. "It's okay, little panther. My name is Snow Flower and this is Remi. We just want to help you."

Snow Flower's soft voice calmed the panther, and he allowed them to approach him. Snow stretched out her hand and the panther sniffed it. "We're going to get you out of this trap," she said calmly. She pulled the chain of the trap while Remi opened it with two sticks. Kuh-chink. The trap came off. But the panther did not run away.

26

"Okay, little one, run along home to your mother now," Snow said playfully as she patted his head.

Then she and Remi gathered their water jugs. They walked to the edge of the forest where it met the road. A swish of leaves startled them again. The panther had followed along. He limped toward them.

"That trap may have hurt his foot," said Remi.

"Maybe we can help him. He seems friendly," replied Snow Flower. She bent down and gave the panther some water from her calabash. Then, she poured the rest onto the grass.

She carefully picked up the young animal and placed him inside the calabash, making sure he was comfortable.

"Let's get him home quickly," said Snow Flower, as she placed the calabash on her head and rushed back to her house with Remi.

"Mamie!" Snow called out to her grandma as they arrived back at the house.

"Yes, Snow?" answered Mamie while she was hanging out the clothes to dry.

"Look what I have in my calabash!"

Mamie turned and was shocked to see what was in the calabash.

"Oh my goodness, Snow! It's a young panther. What made you bring a panther home? It could be dangerous, especially if its mother is near. Where did you find it?"

"He was caught in a hunting trap in the forest. Remi and I freed him. Then he followed us to the road. His leg is injured. So I carried him all the way home."

"Well, you didn't bring the water like I asked, but never mind." Mamie smiled. "I'm glad you're safe and thought to help the panther out. I'll get some bandages."

"I have to go home, but I'm glad the panther is safe," said Remi as he headed toward his house.

Mamie brought out the bandages while Snow lifted the panther out of the calabash. She washed his leg in a bowl of clean water. Mamie dried his leg with a towel and then rubbed some healing ointment onto the wound.

"Do you know, Snow Flower, the panther is our family's animal symbol because of its strength and calmness. Maybe that is why he let you free him and then followed you back. You are strong and calm too."

"Really? I never knew that about our family," said Snow Flower proudly.

She held the panther still while Mamie wrapped a bandage around his leg. After they finished, Snow pet the panther on the head. He purred and his emerald eyes gleamed.

"Good work, Snow," said Mamie. "The panther's wound will heal in a few days and we can carry him back to the forest to be with his family."

Carrying him in her arms, Snow brought the panther into her bedroom. "I think I'm going to call you Nzui," she said. "It means 'panther' in our tribal language."

"Do you say it like this: 'en-zooey'?" the panther asked.

"Wait, you can talk?" Snow said, tripping over her dolls as she stepped back in shock. "How are you able to talk to me?"

"I can talk to you because I can tell you have a pure heart and won't hurt me. My family was captured in the forest by hunters. Now I don't have anywhere to go," Nzui said as he gazed toward the window.

Snow hugged him. "Don't worry, Nzui. Maybe I can help you find them. My grandma knows lots of people in the village and can ask for help. For now, you can stay here with me. You will be safe, I promise."

"Thank you, oh thank you, Snow Flower!" said Nzui. "I'm so happy I can stay. I think we're going to be great friends."

"I think so too," replied Snow as they smiled at each other, imagining the exciting adventures they would have together.